AGENT ARTHUR'S
ISLAND
ADVENTURE

Lesley Sims

Illustrated by Paddy Mounter

Designed by Lucy Parris

Cover design: Russell Punter and Lucy Parris

Edited by Corinne Stockley and Cecily von Ziegesar

Series editor: Gaby Waters

Contents

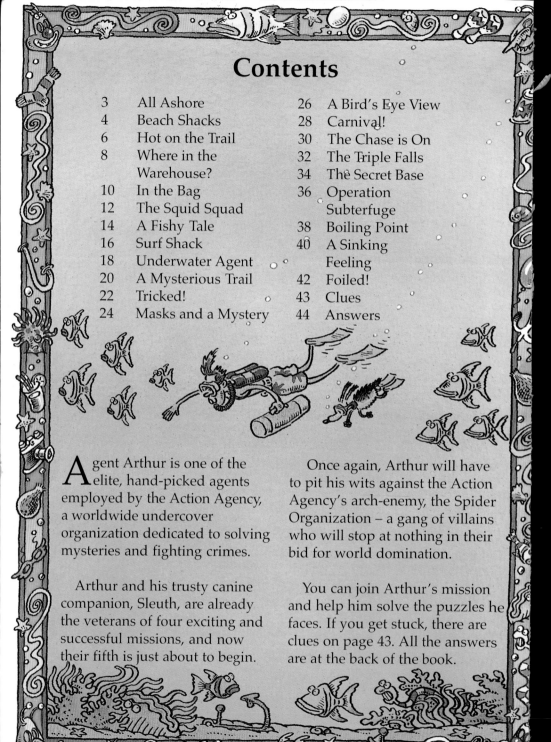

Agent Arthur is one of the elite, hand-picked agents employed by the Action Agency, a worldwide undercover organization dedicated to solving mysteries and fighting crimes.

Arthur and his trusty canine companion, Sleuth, are already the veterans of four exciting and successful missions, and now their fifth is just about to begin.

Once again, Arthur will have to pit his wits against the Action Agency's arch-enemy, the Spider Organization – a gang of villains who will stop at nothing in their bid for world domination.

You can join Arthur's mission and help him solve the puzzles he faces. If you get stuck, there are clues on page 43. All the answers are at the back of the book.

All Ashore

"Mango Island at last!" cried Arthur as he jumped ashore.

A tropical island in the Coral Sea was the last place you'd expect to find trouble. But trouble was why Arthur was here. Not that his instructions told him much. All he knew for certain was that he had to meet the local Action Agent.

"OK, let's act cool," he said, putting on his new Ultra Reflector sunglasses, designed to block out nearly everything. They did. Including the palm tree.

Slightly dazed, Arthur thought back to his mission details, memorized and destroyed in true Agency fashion. How did the code work again? Oh yes, each symbol stood for a vowel.

M¥ss¥øn:
¥nvßst¥g@tß susp¥c¥øµs @ct¥v¥ty øn M@ngø ¥sl@nd by løc@l g@ng thß Squ¥d Squ@d. Løøk øµt før thߥr symbøl. → Bß c@rßfµl. ThBy m@y bß l¥nkßd tø Sp¥dßr Ørg@n¥z@t¥øn.

¥nstrµct¥øns:
Mßßt @gßnt @bß @t thß bß@ch sh@ck w¥th rßd @nd yßlløw str¥pßd røøf @nd grßßn @nd pµrplß t@blßs. Tø m@kß cønt@ct @sk før @ "shr¥mp sµnd@ß".

Can you decipher the code?

Beach Shacks

Arthur and Sleuth soon found the busy part of the beach, packed with people enjoying the sun. There were brightly painted shacks all the way along it – as far as the eye could see, in fact.

"Agent Abe certainly knows how to hide in a crowd," groaned Arthur, as they trudged along. The heat was stifling. His shirt was soaking wet and his feet were stuck to his sandals.

"Still," Arthur continued, "the sooner we find him, the sooner I can get to grips with this mission, not to mention a long, cool drink." Then, just as he spoke, he spotted the right shack.

"Right," said Arthur, snapping into efficient Action Agent mode. "Now we follow our instructions."

Which is the right shack?
What must Arthur do inside?

5

Hot on the Trail

Arthur walked into the Shrimp Shack. "One shrimp sundae, please," he called, climbing onto a shaky stool that toppled over and dumped him on the ground.

"*Shrimp sundae?*" laughed the woman behind the counter. "Here, try this instead." She gave him a plate with a crab on it. "And hold on, I've got a message for you."

Arthur tried a hot and spicy crab claw and wished he hadn't. "Hrrrr!" he gasped, snatching up a handy glass and downing the contents in one gulp.

"Here you are!" said the woman, handing him a coaster with a message on it.

"Sleuth, there's been a change of plan," Arthur hissed. "We have to search for Abe again. He's at his cousin's market stall, but I don't know which one it is. I'll just have to use my keen Agent's instincts."

Arthur – couldn't wait! Meet me at my cousin's stall in the market. Identify yourself with the sentence, "Can a snake samba?" I'll reply, "If a llama can limbo!" and tell you what I've found out so far!
Agent Abe

Soon they were in the market. But which stall belonged to Abe's cousin? Arthur began the search.

They'd missed him again! Still, once Arthur had found a signpost, he knew where to go.

Where is Abe?

Where in the Warehouse?

A hot half-hour later, Arthur and Sleuth reached the warehouse. It was almost deserted – and there was no sign of Abe.

"We could be chasing him all day," said Arthur. "I'm going to start investigating on my own." The trouble was, he had no idea what he was looking for.

"Abe must have had a reason for meeting us *here*," mused Arthur. "Maybe he's found something suspicious."

"The important thing is to look casual," he said, nosing around. "You never know who's watching. Nope, nothing there," he added, waving his hand.

Three crates went flying through the air and crashed to the ground. Arthur jumped back with a yelp and looked around. But nothing else stirred.

Sleuth sniffed the air. The warehouse was full of exciting, fishy smells. But he wasn't sure what to hunt for either.

Arthur, meanwhile, had had enough. "It's no good, we'll *have* to find Abe. Investigating when you don't know what you're investigating, is as much use as a straw hat in a hurricane!" But as he was about to return to the market, he saw something familiar.

What has Arthur spotted?

9

In the Bag

The symbol of the Squid Squad! Arthur opened one of the crates and gingerly put his hand inside. His fingers met something hard and hairy. A coconut!

"Huh?" said Arthur, staring in disbelief. The mission details had talked about "suspicious activity." What was suspicious about *coconuts*? But hang on… maybe this was a cover of some kind. His brain went into overdrive. Coconuts… hard shells… space inside… Inside! What if something was hidden *inside* them?

"Time to lie low somewhere and puzzle this one out," he said, shoving the coconut into his pack. "And I'll take this, too," he added, pulling an envelope off the crate lid and putting it in his pocket.

Then he noticed that the large label on the side of the crate was partly in code. No problem for an Action Agent! He deciphered it quickly and was about to get up when…

FOR MR. CRUSHER
FORT SCAR, MANGO ISLAND

TENTH EGUFRETBUS BATCH
NOITAREPO OF ROF CRATES
DNALSI FROM OGNAM SPIDER
AIV ORGANIZATION DNALSI
HEADQUARTERS REDIPS IN NO
KANGBOK DAUQS TO DIUQS THE

HANDLE WITH CARE!!

...a scratchy, smelly sack was thrown over him. Arthur fought but it was no use. He was picked up and dumped in the back of a truck, followed by the crates.

Twisting around, Arthur managed to force his head up through the rope around the neck of the sack. Doors slammed, wheels squealed and the truck roared off down the road, with Sleuth in hot pursuit. Arthur was thrown all over the truck as it swerved around corners.

Ten hair-raising, hairpin bends later, they screeched to a halt outside some kind of fort. Arthur watched the men carefully unload the crates. Then he was hauled from the truck.

Arthur was bumped down hundreds of steps and locked in a dark, damp cell. If only the Action Handbook had a chapter on *Advice to Agents Flung into Dungeons*, he thought glumly.

Well, it gave him time to think. He knew from the crate label that the Spider Organization *was* involved – and in Operation Subterfuge, whatever that was. I *must* get to the crates' destination as soon as possible, he thought.

Where are the crates being sent?

The Squid Squad

Escape, thought Arthur. But how? Then he noticed a sharp rock jutting out of the wall. In minutes, the sack lay cut to shreds.

Just then, he heard scrabbling noises. Sleuth was burrowing into the cell through crumbling bricks. A disused tunnel lay behind him.

"Ha! An alert Action Agent is never stuck for long," Arthur said, as he crawled up into the tunnel with Sleuth at his heels. They wriggled along, going up and up. All at once, Sleuth growled softly. A light was shining up through a loose grille in the floor. Five men were talking in a gloomy room below them.

"The Squid Squad, I presume," muttered Arthur. "In some kind of guard room," he added, straining to hear what they were saying.

"Now listen," barked out a man with an eye patch. "The *Big Spider*'s meeting us at the Port Papaya Carnival tomorrow. I want you all to be there. But first, final preparations must be made for the launch – that's what he's coming to see. Work all night over there if you have to. When I see the red smoke I'll know everything's ready and you're heading back."

I suppose he must be Crusher, thought Arthur, listening to the man giving orders. Then he spotted a plan of the fort. He studied it carefully.

"We'll climb down through this grille when they go," he whispered. "Now that I know where they'll be, we can sneak through empty rooms to escape."

What is Arthur's escape route?

A Fishy Tale

Safely out in the fresh air again, Arthur spotted a bike leaning against the fort wall. He leapt on and raced off in the direction of the sea front.

"Now to find a way to Spider Island," Arthur panted. He skidded to a stop at a busy quayside.

"Here Sleuth, see if you can crack this," Arthur said, tossing him the coconut he'd brought in his pack. Then he went over to the boats.

"Could someone row me to Spider Island?" he asked. But they just looked at him as if he was crazy. No one would land there.

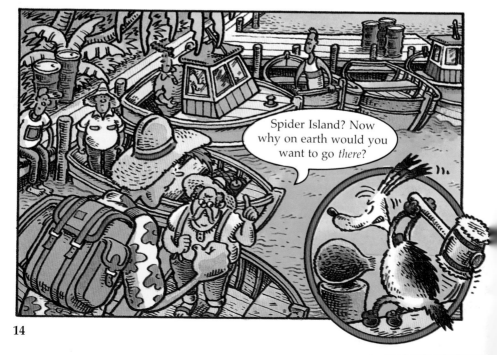

Spider Island? Now why on earth would you want to go *there*?

It used to be a thriving place. Now the mill is deserted and no one lives there. Take my advice – stay away!

You know, there's some say it's cursed.

It was a good place to fish till last year. Then the fish grew sick, and even the sea was murkier . . .

I wouldn't go there for all the fish in the sea. I've seen dark clouds hanging over it. If you ask me, the volcano's about to erupt!

There've been strange goings-on. I've seen lights flashing, and heard some odd rumblings.

Hey, relax! Rent a hammock instead! Mine are cheap!

Old Jonas is the only one who goes near it – but even he only fishes up to the reef.

Surf Shack

Despite all the gloomy warnings, Arthur persuaded Old Jonas to take him as far as the reef around Spider Island.

"Took someone else a few hours ago," Jonas mumbled. "Don't know why the place is suddenly so interesting. Go get yourself some equipment at Solomon's Shack," he added. "You'll need real underwater diving gear to swim through the reef."

Outside the shack, Arthur scanned the goods on display. "Those trunks and that bag look ideal," he said. He studied a map, then noticed a special offer board advertising diving gear. "And there are four things on that special offer board that I'll need too."

Can you find all six items around the shack?

CORAL RESISTANT TRUNKS * *

SURFBOARD FOR SALE! Careful owner!

JOIN RF LUB

SURF B·B·Q Sat 24th.

EXPAND -A WA

Underwater Agent

Wearing his new trunks and diving gear, and with all his things, including the coconut, safely stowed in the waterproof bag, Arthur rejoined Old Jonas. They rowed out to the reef, then Arthur and Sleuth plunged in. Between them and the shore of Spider Island were the nasty creatures shown on Solomon's poster. Arthur had to find a safe way through.

Can you find a route to the shore?

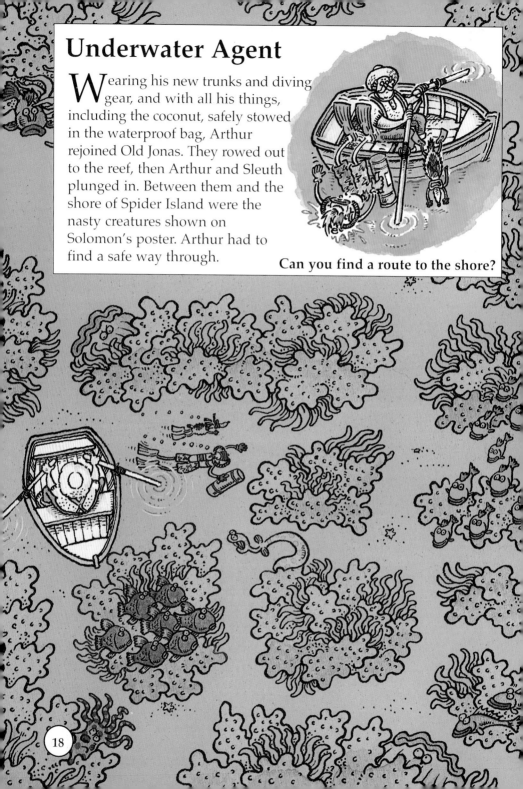

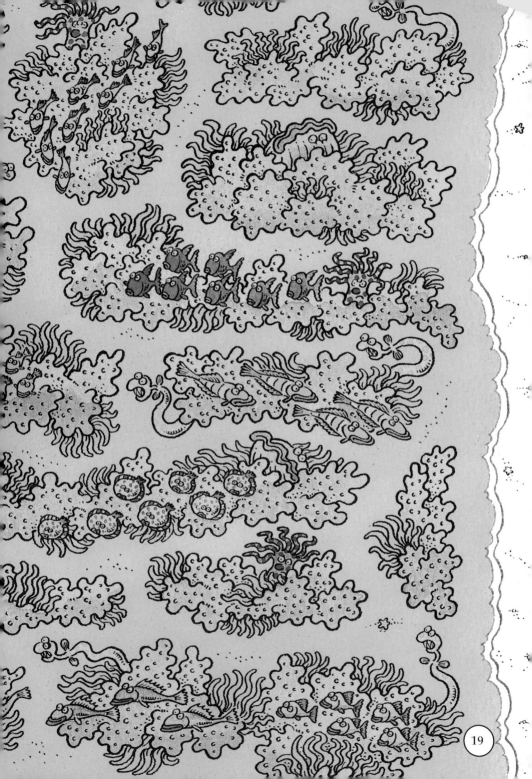

A Mysterious Trail

With a kick of his flippers, Arthur surfaced. He walked cautiously up the sand. This was a dangerous place – the Squid Squad's headquarters was probably not far away.

As he opened his bag, the coconut rolled out. Arthur anchored it with his knee and bashed it with a rock. But *still* the shell wouldn't break.

Sleuth was studying a trail of flipper prints going up the beach. Arthur dressed quickly, and repacked his backpack.

They followed the prints into the undergrowth. Trees grew out at odd angles and strange bushes scratched their legs. A wind was whistling through the palms. Sleuth put his ears on full alert.

The trail was just petering out when Arthur saw a strange sight. Scraps of paper covered in writing were stuck on the spikes of a large cactus. It looked like the wind had blown them there. He carefully put the pieces together to discover a message. Arthur quickly deciphered it.

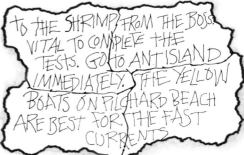

TO THE SHRIMP FROM THE BOSS. VITAL TO COMPLETE THE TESTS. GO TO ANT ISLAND IMMEDIATELY. THE YELLOW BOATS ON PILCHARD BEACH ARE BEST FOR THE FAST CURRENTS.

It made no sense at all. What tests? And where was Ant Island? He looked around but there were no other clues. Nothing but some fish bones, shells and a banana skin, by the smoky remains of a fire.

Someone had had a good lunch, Arthur thought. But something didn't add up. It looked too neat to be litter. In fact, it reminded him of something he'd seen recently… he bent closer and saw a familiar sign in the sand. The 'litter' was a message from Abe!

Giving a shout, he scrambled to the top of the nearest palm tree and looked out to sea. He could see a group of five islands.

"Full speed ahead to the yellow boat on the beach, Sleuth!" Arthur cried. "Abe left us a message on the sand. He's gone to Ant Island, and I know which one that is!"

Do you?

Tricked!

BOOM! As Arthur and Sleuth reached Ant Island, the boat exploded, hurling them onto the shore. Two people ran up to help. Arthur recognized Jane Printz – they had worked together before. But what was she doing *here*?

"Hi! I'm Abe!" said Jane's companion, looking remarkably cheerful. "My boat was booby-trapped too. The Squids set me up with a fake note. I believed every word and came over here on a false trail. I'd show you the fake note, but I tore it up, and– "

"I know, I found the pieces," broke in Arthur, staring in disbelief at his coconut, which had finally broken open in the blast.

"*Huh?*" said Arthur baffled. "I was *sure* something was hidden inside." He told Abe and Jane about the crates at the warehouse.

"There must be something else in those crates," he said. Then he spotted a plane on the beach. "Hey! Whose is this?" he cried.

"Mine!" said Jane. "You're lucky I was passing or you'd be marooned. I was taking photos for a business client and saw Abe's boat explode."

"You know," Jane continued, "when I was taking some shots of that same warehouse earlier, someone told me to stop and tried to steal my camera!"

"Right," Arthur decided. "We'll go straight back to Mango Island and get your film developed." Climbing aboard the plane, he told the others what he'd overheard at the fort.

"If the Squid Squad are meeting the Spider Organization boss at the Port Papaya Carnival, we should be there too," said Arthur. "And this 'launch' must be happening at their headquarters on Spider Island. We must see if we can get in unnoticed."

As the propellers roared, Jane thrust some papers at him. "Will you navigate? Visibility's good, just find the quickest flight path to Mango Island." Arthur rapidly plotted the route.

What is their route and how long will it take?

DISTANCES ARE IN AIRMILES
• DOTS ARE AIRSTRIPS

Ant Island

Port Papaya
Guava City
Mango Island
Spider Island
Tango Town

NOT DRAWN TO SCALE

N

11 7
10 7 7
6 11 8
11 5
9 11
9

Viking Seaplanes

Codes GH201-GH230: Maximum speed 120 airmiles an hour; maximum flying time without stopping to refuel: 10 minutes

Codes GH231-GH260: Maximum speed 60 airmiles an hour; maximum flying time without stopping to refuel: 10 minutes

Airstrip refuel turnaround times:
Pilot + 0-2 passengers: 5 minutes
Pilot + 3 passengers: 15 minutes
Pilot + 4 passengers: 20 minutes
(Passengers include children and pets)

ALL GH AIRCRAFT:
New regulations! Do not attempt sea landings with 2 or more passengers. (Emergency take-offs only!)

23

Masks and a Mystery

Back on Mango Island, Jane hurried off to get her film developed. "Meet me at the Palm Café at five," she called to Arthur.

Abe left too, to send a progress report to the Action Agency, leaving Arthur to shop for carnival costumes – the perfect disguise.

Good spies always blend in with their surroundings, thought Arthur, heading for a festive-looking costume shop.

Out of the corner of his eye, Arthur glimpsed one of the Squid Squad gang who'd kidnapped him earlier.

"Quick! Down here!" Arthur hissed to Sleuth, diving down a side street. A plan showing the route of the carnival procession was stuck on a fence. Arthur studied it closely, while they waited for the Squid to move on.

As soon as the coast was clear, they ran into the shop. It was full of carnival costumes and masks.

Arthur pulled two costumes off a rail, and was looking for a third when he had an amazing stroke of luck. In front of him, pinned to a board full of toothy masks, was a very useful note. Now he knew exactly what the Squid Squad would be wearing!

Just then, a clock struck five. Arthur grabbed the last two masks on the board, and quickly paid for them and the two costumes. The third would have to wait. Jane would be at the café by now – and with pictures someone hadn't wanted her to take. Arthur rushed off.

At the Palm Café, Jane had spread her negatives over the table. "The ones I took at the docks are missing," she told him.

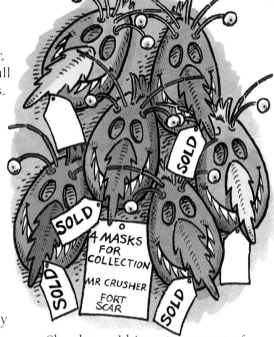

SOLD

SOLD

SOLD

4 MASKS FOR COLLECTION

MR CRUSHER FORT SCAR

SOLD

SOLD

She showed him a torn scrap of negative. "All I have is this. It was stuck to one of the other negatives."

Arthur held the fragment up to the light. "These are the crates I saw," he said. "But something's different."

What has Arthur noticed?

A Bird's Eye View

"When I saw them, they didn't have those MKII codes," Arthur said. "Just the Squid Squad symbol, but... "

As he spoke, Arthur had a brainwave. "Maybe the codes are written in something that only shows up on film. One thing's for sure – those crates are the key to this whole mystery."

"I *must* find the Squid Squad's Spider Island headquarters," he continued. "That's where the crates are being sent. I'll look for it tomorrow, before the carnival."

"By the way," he added, "I've just bought costumes and masks for you and Abe – *and* found out what the Squid Squad's masks will look like!"

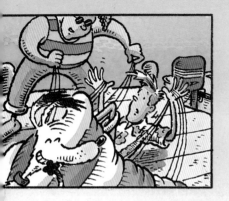

Early the next morning, after a brief paragliding lesson, Arthur was high above Spider Island, with his eyes peeled. It wasn't long before he saw what he thought must be the Squid Squad's headquarters. There was one thing that gave it away.

What was it?

Carnival!

Back on Mango Island, Arthur sketched a map of Spider Island – he *had* to remember the site of that mill. He would have to go there right away.

Jane and Abe were already mingling in the crowd, and Arthur was just about to go and tell them his plans when he saw two of the Squid Squad close by.

He sneaked into the nearest shop, threw down some money, grabbed a clown mask and the costume below it, frantically put it all on and rushed out again.

Outside, he and Sleuth were at once caught up in the carnival mayhem. The streets were packed with people laughing and dancing.

Arthur jigged in the shadow of a girl on stilts as he scanned the crowd. But he couldn't seem to locate any of the four Squid Squad members, let alone Jane or Abe.

Can you find them?

The Chase is On

Arthur froze. One of the Squid Squad was looking straight at him! Luckily his mask did the trick. It was as if Arthur was invisible.

He wondered if the *Big Spider* was here yet, remembering what Crusher had said in the fort. Safe behind his mask, he danced over, hoping to hear something useful.

The crowd surged forward. In the crush, the Squid actually had a hand on Arthur's shoulder, and he *still* didn't know it was Arthur. All that was about to change…

In the space of a second, a man knocked Arthur's mask, the Squid saw him and shouted, and Crusher appeared, shaking his fists.

Arthur fled. Two of the Squid Squad gave chase, but they lost sight of him and Arthur quickly hauled himself aboard the last float, slightly singed by a fire-eater. Looking up at the street names, and remembering the carnival poster he'd seen, he grinned, before turning around to wave. He was safe now.

Why does Arthur think he's safe?

The Triple Falls

The float turned into Salsa Street where two officials were ready with a barrier. Arthur jumped off the float and sped down the road, tearing off his costume as he ran.

Seconds later, footsteps came thudding up behind him. The villains had spotted him and crashed right through the barrier!

Ducking onto Rum Road, Arthur desperately tried to picture the street plan. He held his breath as the men ran past. A frantic game of cat and mouse followed.

Before long Arthur was cornered at the waterfront, outside a café overlooking a thundering waterfall. But he wasn't beaten yet. He ran into the Triple Falls café itself. There was only one way to go. Down!

Everyone stared in disbelief as Arthur grabbed a large tray and threw himself into the waterfall with Sleuth on his back.

Guide to Buoys

Ordinary buoys
Keep starboard buoys on your starboard side and port buoys on your port side.

Port (left) ▢
Starboard (right) ○

Hazard! Avoid the side the dots point to. ⋆̇

Danger! Avoid all four sides. ⋰⋆⋰

Compass buoys
Pass to the north of a north buoy, south of a south one, etc.

N ▢
S ◉
E ▣
W ▢

At the bottom, drenched but unhurt, they crawled across the planking. "We'll take Jonas's boat," Arthur panted to Sleuth, "and get to Spider Island first." On board was a chart covered in symbols, showing a safe landing spot on Spider Island.

On the chart, Arthur marked where they'd be coming in with an arrow. Then he checked the 'symbols guide' in his Action Agent's Handbook to see what the symbols meant, and began to plot the route.

Can you find their route?

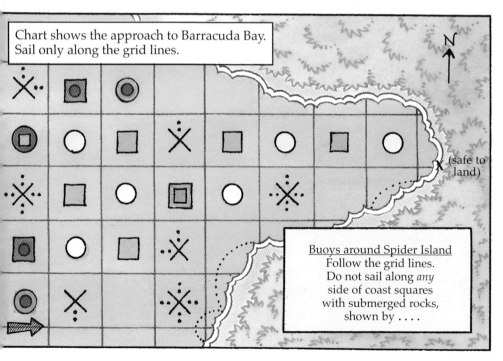

Chart shows the approach to Barracuda Bay. Sail only along the grid lines.

N

X (safe to land)

Buoys around Spider Island
Follow the grid lines.
Do not sail along *any*
side of coast squares
with submerged rocks,
shown by . . . .

The Secret Base

Arthur dragged Jonas's boat onto Barracuda Beach, and checked his soggy hand-drawn map of Spider Island.

"Right, the mill's this way," he told Sleuth. "And we'd better hurry if we're going to snoop around inside before the Squid Squad arrive."

As they went deeper inland, spiky bushes caught them and tangled creepers tripped them up. Precious minutes ticked by while Arthur hacked a way through. But at last the mill was before them. And as he had seen yesterday, it was definitely in use.

The old waterwheel was rusted up, but red smoke was pouring from the chimney and strange noises could be heard coming from inside. Arthur tried the mill door, but it was locked.

"An Action Agent is never at a loss," he muttered, looking around. Up above the waterwheel he saw an open window.

Arthur sprang into mountaineering mode. He reached up, grasped the wheel with both hands and began to climb. Unfortunately, with Arthur's weight on it, it slowly began to move.

Before he knew it, he was in freefall mode. "Aagh!" he cried, as he lost his grip and hurtled to the ground. A few seconds later he came to.

"Ugh, stop that," he told Sleuth, who was licking his face frantically. He stood up, hunting in his pocket for his All-purpose Action Cloth to wipe his damp face. Instead he drew out an envelope.

Of course! It was the envelope he'd torn off the crate, just before he'd been captured at the warehouse. He'd completely forgotten it. He ripped it open and read the letter inside.

Ransom? Poison? <u>Crate production</u>? Were they *making* the crates? How could you hold a city to ransom with *crates?* Arthur had to get to the bottom of it all.

Dear Crusher,
The crate production is going full steam ahead! I'm so glad the Spider Organization agreed to fund us.
Well, zero hour is approaching! I know Tuesday's launch will be successful and then it's all hands to the deck for Marks II and III. On Friday we hold Megacity Port to ransom with Mark I – a taste of what's to come! I hope the containers of extra-poisonous **Deadly Black Gunge®** arrived.
Yours,
Doc Boffin.

But how could he get inside? Then he recalled something he'd seen in the guard room at Fort Scar. Getting in was easy!

How?

Operation Subterfuge

Arthur pressed the J-shaped stone and the door swung open onto a vast chamber, filled with bubbling vats, and hotter than a hundred ovens.

Broken crates lay everywhere. It looked like the Squid Squad were breaking them up, not making them. But why?

Arthur frowned and looked into a vat. It was full of a disgusting yellow concoction, giving off a gas which stung the back of his throat. He choked, tears streaming down his face.

With his vision blurred, Arthur bumped into Sleuth, who fell over a cable. There was a blinding flash. Arthur froze. The cable had come out of a ramshackle generator, but thankfully it still worked when he plugged it back in again.

He leapt to his feet and looked around. Seeing a ladder, he climbed down and found an office with a door at one end, marked 'To the Sub Cave'. On a table was a file of papers, entitled:

OPERATION SUBTERFUGE

At last! thought Arthur. I'll find out what's going on. He opened the file and spread the papers out over the floor. Then he put his Action Speed Reading technique into gear. Two minutes later, he'd learned a lot.

The crates weren't wooden. And the Squid Squad weren't just breaking them up. They were *melting them down*, to make something else. And now Arthur knew what.

Do you?

Boffin Labs

NOTES ON EXPERIMENT 157

Jan 4th: I have just invented a wonderful new material which combines metal and plastic, yet looks like wood. I have named it FLEXIMET.

Jan 5th: Today while working in the lab, I discovered that FLEXIMET is totally undetectable by sonar equipment. This applies to anything behind it too. So a container made of FLEXIMET would be invisible underwater. Imagine it, a FLEXIMET fleet submerged off the coast of every country, threatening to unleash a flood of poison into the seas. I could hold the world to ransom!

Feb 13th: Crusher has suggested we take FLEXIMET to the Spider Organization, since y plan is far too costly for us to set up our own. To make it in the quantities uired, we will need a factory and

CRATE SHIPMENTS

This last batch of crates completes the quantity needed to melt down for Mark I. You should be able to complete it in plenty of time for the scheduled launch day.

NB: the next batch of crates will be marked MKII. The labels will be invisible to the naked eye, as ever.

Code for Security Lock
8 buttons in order beginning top left & finishing bottom right

Boffin Labs
July 30th

My dear Crusher,

I've just discovered something unfortunate about my Clear Propelling Flexifuel.® As you know, once burned up in the engine, Flexifuel® produces a clear non-toxic waste which can be discarded safely. The problem is with the fuel itself. If allowed to mix with water, it undergoes a chemical change which affects FLEXIMET,® making it visible on sonar equipment, so **NEVER** jettison Flexifuel® in range of sonar equipment.

Yours, Doc Boffin.

FAX

To: CRUSHER, BOSS OF THE SQUID SQUAD
From: DOC B.
RE: FLEXIMET®

WARNING: ONE OF MY LAB ASSISTANTS SLIGHTLY OVERHEATED OUR LATEST BATCH OF FLEXIMET.® AFTER TESTS IT PROVED USELESS. THE FLEXIMET® MUST NEVER REACH A TEMPERATURE HIGHER THAN 50°C (122°F). IF IT DOES IT WILL BE UNUSABLE. IF IT GOES TOO HIGH IT MAY EVEN IGNITE AND EXPLODE.

Boiling Point

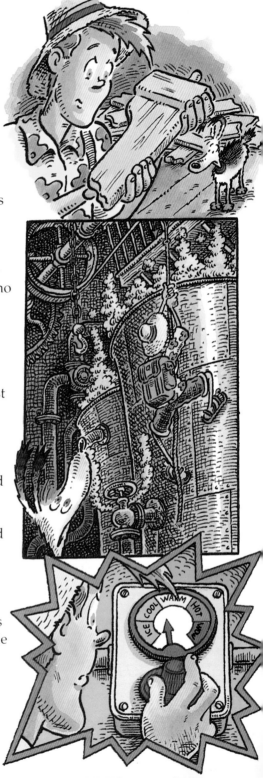

Arthur raced back up the ladder to the room with the vats. Everything was falling into place.

"The crates are made of this Fleximet. They're melted down here and made into invisible submarines!" he muttered. It was a dastardly scheme.

Arthur considered his mission grimly. The Squid Squad and the Spider Organization were up to no good – he had to stop them.

According to the fax he'd just read, Fleximet shouldn't get too hot. So all he had to do was turn up the heat in the vats to full blast and the Squid Squad's plans would be utterly foiled.

Set on sabotage, he frantically looked around. Finally he spotted the thermostat – part of a giant control panel, on a balcony half-way up a wall. Quickly, he pulled out his Reach-All Action Grappling Hook and swung it at the balcony. Would it hold? Yes!

Checking to see if the rope was taut, he shot up it, scaling the side of a vat. Once on the balcony, he turned the heat on full blast. The stuff in the vats bubbled away more violently than ever.

Then the awful realization hit him. In the fort, the boss had said the Big Spider was coming for a launch. It could mean only one thing. Submarine Mark I was built and ready to go!

He spun around to climb back down and knocked his hook off the rail. It plummeted into the vat below. "Oh no, what next?" he groaned, pulling on his gloves.

A tangle of pipes covered the room from ceiling to floor. He'd have to use those, even though it meant going perilously close to the vats.

As he climbed, he thought fast. Where was the submarine? A phrase nagged at the back of his mind. Of course! The 'Sub Cave' – where else?

Arthur scrambled back down the ladder to the door in the office – but it was locked electronically. The buttons on the keypad had shapes which looked like they might be significant.

Recalling the code he'd seen in the file, he hit the top left button first, then the remaining buttons needed to unlock the door.

What is the right sequence?

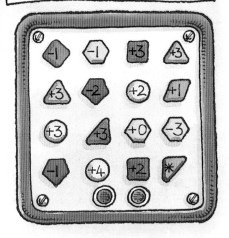

TEST LAUNCH SITE
To open the door, key in the security code. No button to be pressed more than once. Buttons must be next to each other, horizontally, vertically or diagonally.

A Sinking Feeling

The door opened onto stone steps. Arthur and Sleuth flew down them and found the submarine, floating silently.

As Arthur looked around, Sleuth gave a warning growl. Seconds later, they heard footsteps and angry voices.

"How could you *LOSE* him?"

"What could we do, huh? He went right over the waterfall in front of us. Anyway, he couldn't have survived, he probably… "

"Oh, shut up!" Arthur heard Crusher say. "Mr. Big Spider sir, if you'd go down there, sir, we've set up a special remote control for the test launch, sir."

Arthur didn't waste any more time. He and Sleuth leapt onto the submarine and jumped in through the entry hatch. They didn't even stop to shut it.

A man in a white suit and red glasses strode into the cave, followed by the Squid Squad.

"The orange button will sink the sub sir," said Crusher. "Then we'll activate the sonar scanner. If you watch this screen here, you'll see the sub become invisible!"

The Big Spider was about to press the button when he stopped and pointed. "Should that entry hatch be open?" he asked. Arthur held his breath. Would they guess he was inside? No, Crusher barked out an order to close it. Arthur sighed with relief as the hatch slammed shut.

He stared dejectedly at the levers on the sub's control panel: Poison Release, Fuel Release... He'd never failed on a mission before... And he wasn't about to fail this time either. All at once, he saw how to sabotage the test.

What can he do?

MARK I

Foiled!

Crusher and the rest of the Squid Squad watched in horror as the submarine shape stayed on the screen. As the fuel seeped out underwater, the Fleximet was rendered useless. Their plan lay in ruins.

The Big Spider was furious. "I knew this would never work!" he ranted. "I said it was crazy! We won't be wasting any more money on you," he finished angrily.

"There's been some mistake," the boss gabbled. "We followed Boffin's instructions to the letter."

"The mistake was working with you," snapped the Big Spider. "This Fleximet is a total failure. As of now, the project's terminated! You'll never work with the Spider Organization again!"

The Big Spider stormed out, followed by two of the Squid Squad and a cringing Crusher.

Meanwhile, Submarine Mark I slowly resurfaced. Arthur opened the entry hatch a little way and listened. Silence. The cave was empty. His sabotage had worked!

But as he began to climb out, his heart sank. Two of the Squid Squad were still there and, what was worse, they were waving threateningly.

Just then, the submarine started to shake. In seconds, the whole island was shaking too. What was happening?

Suddenly, Arthur remembered the dangers of overheating Fleximet. "If we don't leave *now,* we'll be blown up!" he hissed.

If only he could have seen them from behind, Arthur would have known what Sleuth's nose had told him already. These two Squids were no threat.

Why not?

Clues

Pages 4-5
See Arthur's instructions on page 3.

Pages 6-7
Draw a simple map on squared paper showing the market and the places around it. Then follow Abe's route.

Pages 8-9
Look carefully at every crate.

Pages 10-11
Read to the end and back again.

Pages 12-13
Arthur is above the guardroom.

Pages 16-17
He won't need the harpoon, the weights or the snorkel.

Pages 18-19
Arthur can swim past the seaweed and the fish.

Pages 20-21
The banana skin is Spider Island.

Pages 22-23
The plane's code is GH237, so it travels at one airmile a minute.

Pages 24-25
Look at the crates on pages 8-9.

Pages 26-27
What did Crusher say on page 13?

Pages 28-29
Check the masks on page 25.

Pages 30-31
Read all the information on the poster on page 24.

Pages 32-33
Remember to stay on the lines.

Pages 34-35
Read the notice board in the guard room on page 13.

Pages 36-37
Study Doc Boffin's 'Notes on Experiment 157'.

Pages 38-39
The first button has 4 sides and says -1. The second button he presses has 3 sides. Could there be a connection?

Pages 40-41
Look again at Doc Boffin's letter on page 37. What has he discovered about Flexifuel?

Page 42
Look again at the masks on page 25, then look in through a window on page 31.

Answers

Page 3

Decoded, a = @, e = ß, i = ¥, o = ø and u = μ.

The two sheets read:

Mission: Investigate suspicious activity on Mango Island by local gang the Squid Squad. Look out for their symbol. →✦ Be careful. They may be linked to Spider Organization.

Instructions: Meet Agent Abe at the beach shack with red and yellow striped roof and green and purple tables. To make contact ask for a 'shrimp sundae'.

Pages 4-5

The shack Arthur must visit is shown below.

He must order a 'shrimp sundae'.

Pages 6-7

Abe is waiting at the warehouse. The route he took is shown in red:

├──┤ 1m

N ↑

• Market

• Warehouse
• Docks

Pages 8-9

Three crates have the symbol of the Squid Squad on them, first seen on Arthur's mission details on page 3.

Pages 10-11

The crates are going to Spider Island. To decipher the label, read every other word from top left to bottom right, starting with the first word. Then read the remaining words back, from bottom right to top left. These words have also been written back to front. Decoded, the crate label reads:

TENTH BATCH OF CRATES FROM SPIDER ORGANIZATION HEADQUARTERS IN KANGBOK TO THE SQUID SQUAD ON SPIDER ISLAND VIA MANGO ISLAND FOR OPERATION SUBTERFUGE

Pages 12-13

From the guard room, Al and Ben will go to the boat room, then the jetty, and will leave by boat. Col and Crusher will go to the meeting room and Dan to the fax room. Arthur and Sleuth can climb down into the guard room, but they must go straight into the laundry room, as Crusher will be coming back through the guard room in only a few seconds. Once Dan has gone to the radio room, followed by Crusher, Arthur and Sleuth can follow their path through the fax room, then the weapons room, through the hall, and leave by the main exit.

Pages 16-17

The trunks, bag and four other things can be found as shown:

Trunks   Mask   Gloves

Flippers

Air tank   Bag

Pages 18-19

Arthur's route to the shore is shown in black.

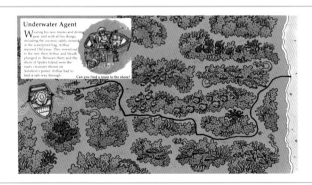

Pages 20-21

Abe has made a map from things he found on the beach. The banana skin is Spider Island. The 5 islands to the north of Spider Island are shown by 4 shells and a fish bone cross. The cross must be Ant Island.

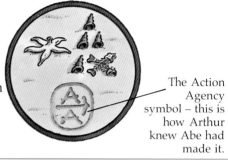

The Action Agency symbol – this is how Arthur knew Abe had made it.

Pages 22-23

The fastest possible route is shown in red. The plane (code GH237) flies 60 airmiles an hour (maximum), which is one airmile per minute. Their

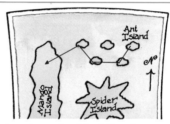

maximum flying time before stopping to refuel is 10 minutes, so they can fly 10 airmiles before stopping to refuel. Each airstrip stop adds 15 minutes to the time (for a pilot + 3 passengers), so their journey takes 74 minutes (1 hour and 14 minutes).

Pages 24-25

When Arthur saw the crates at the docks, they did not have any 'MK II' codes on them, under the Squid Squad symbols.

Pages 26-27

The "deserted" mill is obviously being used. And there's red smoke coming out of the chimney. In the guard room on page 13, Crusher talked about a red smoke signal.

Pages 28-29

The members of the Squid Squad are circled in black. Arthur is circled in red, Jane and Abe in blue.

Pages 30-31

Arthur has seen the sign for Salsa Street and remembers a note on the poster on page 24. At the end of the parade, the street will be blocked to everyone except floats and he has jumped aboard the last one.

Pages 32-33

Their route is shown in red.

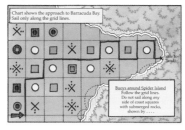

Pages 34-35

To enter the mill Arthur must press this J-shaped stone.

He saw this note on the board in the guardroom on page 13.

Pages 36-37

The Squid Squad are making submarines which are invisible to sonar scanning equipment. The submarines are being made from **Fleximet** – a new material invented by Doc Boffin (a friend of Crusher, the Squid Squad leader). It looks like wood but is actually a mixture of metal and plastic.

The **Fleximet** is made in Doc Boffin's lab in Kangbok and sent to the Squid Squad as crates. These are melted down, re-shaped and built into submarines. Because the crates are for different submarines, they are marked with codes in infrared labels (invisible to the naked eye) so the Squid Squad know which crate is for which submarine.

The Squid Squad are being funded by the Spider Organization, who intend to use the submarines to hold the world to ransom. The submarines will be filled with **Deadly Black Gunge**, and positioned in seas around the world. The Spider Organization will threaten to poison the oceans unless their demands are met.

Pages 38-39

The full sequence is shown here. The numbers on the buttons refer to the number of sides on the next shape in the sequence. The card from the file (shown on page 37) says press 8 buttons, starting top left. This has 4 sides and says -1, so the next button is the triangle below it. The sequence ends with the star key, bottom right.

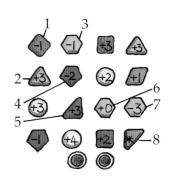

Pages 40-41

All Arthur has to do is pull the Fuel Release lever, emptying the fuel tanks. As the Flexifuel floods out, the submarine will appear on the sonar screen. In a letter Doc Boffin sent to Crusher (on page 37) the Doc described a serious problem with Flexifuel. In water, it makes Fleximet visible to sonar scanners.

Page 42

The two "members" of the Squid Squad are none other than Jane and Abe. On pages 28 and 29, you can see them enjoying the carnival, in the masks Arthur found on page 25.

They captured the real Squid Squad gang members on page 31. You can see Jane with their prisoners through this window.